Secret
of the Pyramid

Penn Mullin

High Noon Books
Novato, California

D1506714

Cover Design and Interior Illustrations: Nancy Peach

International Standard Book Number: 1-57128-057-X

10 09 08 07 06 05 04 03 02 01
9   8   7   6   5   4

You'll enjoy all the High Noon Books.
Write for a free full list of titles.

Contents

Corina and Zack are young co-workers at the Park Museum. They are assistants to the museum's director, Claire Long, who sends them to the "four corners of the world" on exciting explorations.

CHAPTER 1

A Hidden Tomb!

"How would you like to go inside a pyramid?" asked Claire.

"Yes!" Corina and Zack answered together. "When?" Claire was the boss at the Park Museum where they worked. She had called them into her office for a special meeting.

"Right away! I just had an e-mail message in secret code from my friend Zia in Egypt. She works for the Cairo Museum and thinks she has found the entrance to a hidden tomb! It is deep inside a pyramid," Claire said. "She wants me with her when she first goes into the tomb."

"Why don't you go?" Corina asked.

"I'd love to. But can you see me crawling through a tunnel on my hands and knees with this broken ankle?" Claire laughed.

"Why can't she wait till you get out of your cast?" Zack asked.

"There is a big problem with tomb robbers in Egypt," Claire explained. "Just like there was 4000 years ago! It's hard keeping it a secret when a new tomb is found. That's why Zia has to move fast on this new discovery!"

"So you want us to go there in your place?" Corina asked. She sounded excited.

"Yes, I do," Claire smiled. "Can you be ready to leave for Cairo by Saturday? Zia plans to go into the tomb on Monday."

"We'll be ready!" Corina said. "Which king's tomb is it?"

"It belonged to the pharaoh called Khufa (KOO-fa). He was king of Egypt over 4000 years ago. He died very young and his pyramid was never finished," Claire said. "People thought his body had been stolen because his stone coffin in the pyramid was empty. But now Zia may have found his real tomb! The *real* resting place of his mummy. You two may see history being made."

CHAPTER 2

A *Felucca* on the Nile

"I hope we're in the right place," Zack said to Corina. "This is where the guy is supposed to meet us for the trip to the pyramid."

It was Monday afternoon in Cairo, the capital city of Egypt. Corina and Zack stood on the dock by the Nile river. Crowds of people were pushing towards a line of boats.

"How will he ever find us?" Corina said. "We should be wearing signs or something."

"Maybe we're the only ones on the dock

who look lost," Zack laughed.

"Corina and Zack?" A short, wiry young man hurried up to the tall dark-haired pair waiting on the dock.

"Yes! That's us!" Corina smiled. "Are you Calide (ca-LEED), Zia's friend?"

"I am. Please just call me Cal. Welcome to Cairo. I hope you had a good flight from America." Cal's smile lit up his whole face. "Let me help you with your bags. We'll go get on the *felucca*."

"Is that the boat?" Zack asked.

"Yes, the Nile tour boats are called *feluccas* (fa-LOO-cas). I am glad you will get to ride on one. It is beautiful on the Nile."

5

Corina and Zack followed Cal onto the felucca. The boat was about 75 feet long with beautiful tall sails. The three sat down on long benches on the deck.

Zack leaned his tall thin body back in the deck chair. "Oh, does this feel good! We left a blizzard in America."

"I sure wish Claire could have come, too," Corina said. "She really wanted to share in Zia's big discovery." Corina picked up her laptop computer and unzipped it. "I should e-mail her and tell her we met up with Cal."

Cal said softly, "I think we should be very careful when we talk. We don't want the wrong people to hear about the tomb. It is important to

Corina and Zack followed Cal onto the felucca. The boat was about 75 feet long with beautiful tall sails.

keep it top secret. Should you talk about the tomb on the Internet?"

"We have a code we use with Claire to talk about the tomb," Corina told him. "That way no one can find out anything."

"Good," said Cal. "Zia will meet us at the pyramid. It is not far away."

"Here we go!" Zack said. The boat's engines rumbled underneath them. A few people jumped aboard just at the last minute.

"How far does this *felucca* go on the Nile?" Corina asked Cal.

"All the way down to the dam at Aswan. That takes fourteen days," Cal said. "The Nile flows on south farther into Africa after that. Did you know it is the longest river in the world – 4,000 miles!"

"Wow! We'll just see a very small part of it. We get back on this boat tomorrow and take it down to the Valley of the Kings," Corina said. "I've always wanted to see King Tut's tomb. And Claire gave us some time off to sightsee."

"I can't believe the treasures they found in Tut's tomb. A coffin made of solid gold!" Zack said. "Not bad for a guy only 19 years old!"

"Tut's is one of the only tombs the grave robbers missed," Cal said. "Probably because it was so well hidden in the side of a mountain. Those tombs in the rocks were harder for robbers to find than pyramid tombs."

"Look! There are the three pyramids and the sphinx we saw from the plane," Corina said. "They're right at the edge of the city!"

"Aren't they beautiful?" said Cal. "They were built around 2500 B.C. as tombs for three different kings. The largest is 450 feet high. It's made of 2½ million stone blocks."

"Amazing!" Zack whistled. "I just can't picture how they ever lifted the stones up there. How much did the stones weigh?"

"About 2½ tons each!" said Cal. "The stones arrived by boat on the Nile. Then they were dragged up to the pyramid. Ramps went around the pyramids. They greased these with water so men could push the stones up and into

10

*"Look! There are the three pyramids and the sphinx
we saw from the plane. They're right at the
edge of the city!"*

place."

"How long did it take to build a pyramid?" Corina asked.

"Some people say 20 years," Cal told her. "With 10,000 men working. But no one can be sure. The pyramids are great mysteries."

The *felucca* moved slowly along the Nile. Bright green fields of vegetables lined the banks. Beyond the green was the wide, endless desert. Children fished from the river shore and waved as the boat passed by.

"The Nile used to be full of crocodiles," Cal said. "You can see pictures of them in the Book of the Dead."

"Book of the Dead?" Corina stared at him.

CHAPTER 3

The Pyramid of Khufa

"The 'Book of the Dead' was always buried with a person in old Egypt," Cal said. "It told secrets of how to have endless life. It gave the dead the answers to questions they would be asked at the door of the afterworld."

"The afterlife was really important to the Egyptians," Corina said. "Didn't they put everything in with the person that they would need in the afterlife – food, clothing, jewelry, animals, even furniture?"

"That's right," said Cal. "And they put tiny boats into the tomb, too. They believed that you traveled to the afterworld by boat. Kings' bodies were always carried to the tomb by boats on the Nile," Cal explained. "The boats would dock near the pyramid. Just the way we are about to do now."

The boat's engines were slowing down. Corina and Zack could see a dock up ahead.

"Is that where we're going – Khufa's tomb?" Corina asked. She looked over towards the pyramid standing alone in the desert.

"Yes. We get off here. Now is a good time to arrive. The tourists are mostly gone from the pyramid," Cal told them softly.

They began walking up to the road to the pyramid in the growing darkness.

"This is the same path they used to pull King Khufa's mummy up towards his tomb," Cal told them. "Picture a long parade of people following his huge coffin, still on its boat! And they brought with them all the treasures their king might need in the afterlife."

"I bet the tomb robbers didn't waste any time after the tombs were sealed," Zack said.

"You're right. It was amazing how they found their way into these tombs," Cal said softly. "And still do."

"The closer we get, the larger the pyramid is," Corina said. "Now I can see how the sides aren't really smooth at all. The stones are like little steps going up."

"And look how the top of the pyramid is not quite pointed," said Cal. "That's because Pharaoh Khufa died before it was finished. The workers had to leave and start work on a tomb for the new Pharaoh!"

"No loyalty!" laughed Zack.

Now the pyramid stood out huge and dark against the red sky behind it. Everything was quiet. Was Zia somewhere nearby? They could see the lights of a small building off in the distance. Suddenly the lights went out and a figure came out of the house towards them.

CHAPTER 4

The Graverobbers' Way

"Welcome, I'm Zia," said the small, beautiful black-haired woman who came up to them. "And you must be Corina and Zack. Claire tells me so much about you!"

"We hope it all was good!" laughed Corina. "Claire sends you her love."

"I wish she could have come, too. Too bad about that ankle." Zia's voice lowered. "But I'm so glad you two are here and can tell Claire about all of this. I think Cal and I have found something wonderful. But before we start, I need to check with security. Cal, will you take their bags over to my building for safekeeping?"

Zia pulled out a small cellular phone from her pocket and spoke softly into it. Her eyes looked all around the base of the pyramid as she talked. Cal ran over to the dark building with the bags and the laptop.

"O.K.," Zia said when she turned off the phone. "Things look good. The guards are watching this whole area."

Cal returned with backpacks for Corina, Zack, and himself. Zia already wore hers.

"There are headlamps to strap on and water bottles in there," Cal told them. "Some candy bars, too. Better not take cameras. This still has to be kept secret."

"Before we go in, I want to tell you a few things," Zia whispered to Corina and Zack. "We are going to go in on the north side of the pyramid. The tunnel was first made by grave-robbers 4,000 years ago! They got partway in and then gave up. This was lucky for us. They tried another entrance and found an empty coffin and no treasures."

"We think what they found was a fake tomb," Cal said. "They were supposed to think someone had already been there and robbed the tomb before them. Very clever plan. So the real tomb stayed hidden."

"And we *hope* hidden until tonight," whispered Zia. "Well, are we ready?"

"Yes," said Corina and Zack together.

Zia and Cal started off towards one side of the pyramid in the darkness. Corina and Zack followed close behind. Where would the tunnel entrance be? Suddenly Zia and Cal stopped at a huge boulder near the pyramid. Cal bent down and moved a large flat stone aside. Then he shined his flashlight down towards the ground.

Zia waved at them to come over. They looked into the hole that went down into the darkness. Its opening was about four feet wide. How deep was it? How long?

"Don't worry," whispered Cal. "It's only 6

feet deep here. Then it turns and goes down under the pyramid. We'll have the headlamps on the whole time down there. I'll go in first, then Corina, you follow me."

"You can go after Corina, Zack, and I'll be last," Zia said. "We'll just take our time." She took her headlamp out of her pack but did not turn it on.

Cal looked carefully around the pyramid area as he knelt down by the hole. The only sound was a soft wind in the air.

Will the guards come and watch the hole after we've gone down? Zack wondered. Where *are* the guards? There was only silence. And it was time to go. Cal was lowering himself feet first into the dark hole.

"When you touch bottom, kneel down and feel for the side tunnel," Cal whispered to Corina. "Then turn on your headlamp and follow me." Suddenly Cal's head disappeared into the hole and he was gone.

"See you down there." Corina smiled and gave Zack a high five. She strapped on her light and started to lower her feet into the hole. "Don't worry," Zia said. "The tunnel gets bigger as you go."

Corina felt the tunnel walls closing around her. Would her feet ever touch the bottom? There – she could feel stone under her. She turned on her flashlight and dropped to her knees. There was a side tunnel. Just where Cal had said. She could see Cal's light a little way down the tunnel. She knew she had to follow him, but the tunnel seemed so small. Slowly she began to pull herself along. The rock under her felt cold and damp.

"I'm right here," Cal called back to her. "Just keep coming. The tunnel gets bigger."

Corina could hear Zack sliding down into the hole behind her.

"I'm down!" he called to Corina. "Hey, being tall doesn't help in these tunnels. Those graverobbers must have been short guys!" Zack got down on his knees and flattened himself out to crawl. He could hear Zia starting to let herself down behind him.

Corina crawled along behind Cal. All she could think of was the graverobbers who dug the tunnel. What if there was a skeleton in here? How much farther did this tunnel go?

"We're under the pyramid now. The tunnel is getting bigger," Cal called back to her.

Yes, the tunnel was larger now. Suddenly Cal held out his hand and pulled her out into a small room cut from solid rock. It felt great to stand up again.

"We made it!" Cal smiled warmly at Corina. "That was the hardest part, I promise!"

Cal gave a hand to help Zack into the room, too. "Watch your head!" he warned. "This place was not made for tall people!"

Soon they were all four standing in the small room. "This was as far as the robbers got in their digging," Zia said. "Lucky for us they gave up here. I think they knew they were somewhere near the tomb, though. Look at this!" She pointed to a large wooden hammer stuck into the wall between two huge rocks. "They were trying to force an opening there."

"It's still stuck there after 4,000 years!" Zack said. "Unbelievable!"

Zia tapped on the rock wall of the room with a hammer. "Hear that sound? Hollow behind this wall. There's a room there. And I think it's the tomb!"

CHAPTER 5

At the End of the Tunnel

Zia and Cal took out more hammers and picks from their backpacks. They quickly began pounding on the rock wall.

"I don't think the rock is too thick here," Cal said. "It won't take us long to break through."

"Amazing!" said Corina. "We're about to step into a tomb no one has been in for 4,000 years!"

"We *hope*." Zia said excitedly. "We can't be sure till we get into the tomb. Often the robbers have gotten there first." She and Cal kept pounding away at one small part of the wall. Suddenly there was a new sound. An echo! Zia's pick had broken through! And the echo came from a large space on the other side!

"We did it!" yelled Cal. Cold air rushed out of the hole. He and Zia took turns with Corina and Zack, chipping away at the small hole.

"My hands are shaking, I'm so excited!" Zia said. She pressed her eyes to the hole and shined her flashlight into it.

"What do you see? Tell us!" Cal was trying to see through the hole, too.

"Wait – it's so dark. But there – I can see better now," Zia said. "Yes! It's the tomb. We really found it! There's *gold* – everywhere! Look!" She stepped aside for the others.

Zack's turn came. He whistled. "This is amazing. They packed *everything* in there for their king. I can see chairs, couches, tables, even a chariot! Corina, look at this!"

Corina peered into the hole. Her flashlight was shining on a huge gold throne. She gasped. *Everything* was gold! Dazzling!

"You're going to be famous," Zack told Zia and Cal. "The whole world is going to want to see this."

"Let's get in there," said Cal. They all started chipping away at the rock.

Soon the hole was big enough for them all

to squeeze through. One by one they crawled out of the hole into the tomb. They stood and stared around them. No one spoke.

Finally Zia whispered, "We're the first people to see this in 4,000 years. I feel dizzy! I never thought we'd ever find anything like this. Untouched. The family who buried Khufa sealed his tomb until this very moment.

They began to explore the large room. It was crowded with furniture, large golden jewelry boxes, chairs, jars of food and wine. All gifts for the king to use in his new life.

"What about the entrance they used to bury Khufa?" Corina asked. "Where is it?"

"They sealed the tomb entrance as they

left. But it's here somewhere."

"Look at the logs up there!" said Cal. "They've held up the ceiling for 4,000 years!"

"And these paintings on the walls!" Zack went up to a drawing of a young man hunting birds with a spear. "This must have been Khufa himself when he was alive."

"Yes, the Egyptians drew pictures of the dead person doing something he liked to do," said Cal. "And pictures of what the person would enjoy in the afterlife."

"Look – here are spears for Khufa to use in his hunting," Corina said. "I wonder why he died so young."

"We don't know. But now maybe the

"The Egyptians drew pictures of the dead person doing something he liked to do. And pictures of what the person would enjoy in the afterlife."

hieroglyphics in this tomb will tell us," Cal answered. He pointed at the tiny pictures and symbols written in lines along the walls.

"Can you read them?" Corina asked.

"Not well. But Zia can," Cal said.

"Sometimes. But I usually need my notes to help me." Zia walked up close to the wall and looked at the picture writing. "It seems that Khufa *was* quite a hunter. So much here talks about this. "May the Pharaoh have good hunting, many birds, sharp spears.' Then I can't read the next line. But when I bring my notes I'll be able to tell you why he died!"

"Look – the sarcophagus!" Cal stood in front of a huge stone box at the end of the room.

It was covered with fine carvings.

"Well, here you are at last, Pharaoh Khufa!" Zia said softly. "I've been looking for you a long time." She reached up to touch the beautiful stone case that held the young Pharaoh's body.

"The lid must weigh over 3 tons," Cal said. "We'll need to bring in special tools to open it."

"How many coffins are inside the sarcophagus?" Zack asked.

"Well, remember that the Egyptians believed their kings turned into gods after death. So they buried them in the very finest way. Khufa's mummy is inside a kind of nest of coffins," Zia explained. "An inner one, a second one, and a third outer one. You will see when we open Khufa's tomb."

"Yes, you must stay longer and be here when we see the mummy," Cal said.

"It is amazing how well the bodies are preserved," Zia told them. "The Egyptians were masters at this. Did you know it took 70 days to prepare a mummy? First they took out the inner organs of the body, like the brain. They put these in separate jars. Like these here." Zia pointed to some large round jars.

"Then they dried the body with chemicals," Cal said. "By now it was quite small. They covered the body with jewels and rare stones. Then they began wrapping it in layers of linen cloth. After 20 layers, the mummy's body was normal size again.'

"The last thing they did was cover the head with a painted mask that looked like the person. Like the famous golden one on King Tut's mummy," said Zia.

"We must stay longer and be here when you open the sarcophagus!" Corina said.

"For sure," Zack said. "I know Claire will agree. As she said, this is *history*."

"All of these treasures will go to our museum in Cairo," said Zia. "They belong to the people of Egypt. We must keep this tomb a secret until the treasures are safely there."

"Right. The sooner, the better," said Cal.

"We'd better start out. But it's hard to leave this place."

"Yes," Zia said. "After waiting so long to get here!"

Cal crawled into the tunnel first to lead the way out. Corina followed him, then came Zack and Zia. It all seems easier now, thought Corina. Not so scary and unknown.

Suddenly there was a strange sound ahead in the tunnel – like rocks and sand falling!

Corina's heart began to pound. Was the tunnel caving in?

Cal had stopped. "Wait!" was all he said.

Now sand was falling on their heads. Were they going to be buried alive down here?

CHAPTER 6

Fear in the Night!

"Nobody move!" Cal yelled. "Let the little stuff come down. We'll be O.K. We'll keep going. Inch by inch. This tunnel is very fragile. But I think it will hold. Just sit tight."

"You O.K., Corina?" Zack called from behind her.

"I think so," she answered. Did her voice sound as scared as she felt?

"These old tunnels are tricky," Zia said. "You just have to let them grumble and complain a bit. I'm calling the guards on the cell phone. Just so they'll know what's going on."

Zack felt the sweat running down his forehead. Was Zia scared, too, and just trying to make them feel better? The tunnel walls felt like they were squeezing him tighter and tighter. How long would they have to stay down here?

Cal's body was totally motionless. Sand was still sifting down, but much less of it now. "We'll wait a few more minutes," he said.

No one moved. They just listened for the sand. And rocks. But finally the tunnel was quiet again.

"O.K.," Cal said. "Everybody move *slowly*. Inch by inch. Don't let your body touch the tunnel walls or ceiling. Let's go. *Slowly*."

They began to inch their way out behind Cal. Every minute or so sand would start to sift down again. Everyone froze. Then they would start again. On and on. Inch by inch.

"Everybody O.K.?" Zia called out softly.

"Yes! O.K.," came back the tired voices from the tunnel.

"Not much farther now," Cal gasped. "We've almost got it made. Just go slow."

Suddenly sand fell down onto Zack's face! Into his eyes and mouth, choking him. He tried to cry out but couldn't.

Corina heard the sand fall. "Cal, wait!" She called. "Zack, you O.K.?"

Zack spit out sand and wiped his eyes. I'm O.K. Let's just keep going."

No more sand was falling now. They inched on down the tunnel. Zack kept coughing on the sand he had swallowed. He could feel the sand in his ears and nose, too. On and on they crawled. Would the tunnel ever end?

Suddenly Corina gasped. Something *alive* had fallen on her neck! She froze. Whatever it was crawled under her shirt! She could feel its tiny legs on her skin! "Wait!" Corina yelled. She had to get it out of her shirt – whatever it was. But how? She couldn't stand up. She shook her body and started to undo her shirt.

"What's wrong?" Zack called to her.

"Something fell down my back! I can't get it out!"

"A lizard. They love these tunnels," Zia said. "Stay still. He'll get off of you."

Corina stopped moving. She could feel the lizard creeping down her back. It was horrible. She wanted to scream. Suddenly it slithered out of her shirt. It vanished into the darkness.

"He's gone," Corina said weakly. "That was awful. Let's get out of here."

On and on they crawled through the tunnel. At last Cal called out, "We made it! But don't rush – go slow. It could still fall. The guards will pull us up in a minute."

Just a few more feet to go. It was hard to

go slow now. They just wanted to be *out*! More sand came down. They stopped. Held their breath. Started again.

Now Cal was being pulled up by a rope. Then Cal lowered it down to Corina to grab. The cool night air felt wonderful as she came up onto the desert again. Safe! But she couldn't stop her body from shaking. The guards wrapped blankets around each of them.

"Drink water," Zia told them all. "As much as you can hold." They stood in a circle with their blankets around them.

Finally Corina felt herself stop shaking. She began to relax. Then she could talk.

"That was really scary," she whispered.

"Yes, you're right!" Cal said. "But I was pretty sure the tunnel would hold."

"Only *pretty* sure? I'm glad you didn't tell us that." Corina smiled. "You did a great job getting us out. Thanks, Cal."

They all grinned at each other then. And suddenly they could think about the tomb again – the amazing treasures they had found. They knew they had made history tonight. But for now they had to keep it a secret.

"I'll have a heavy guard placed here at the tunnel," said Cal.

"Then we can all get some food and rest. Corina and Zack, we have rooms for you in a hotel nearby," Zia said. "Rest tomorrow. Then you can take the boat down the Nile to King Tut's tomb. It will take a while to make a new passageway into this tomb. When you come back, maybe we can go in and open the sarcophagus!"

"Is it O.K. to e-mail Claire about the tomb?" Corina asked Zia. "We'd use the code so it would be secret."

"Yes, and tell her she must come to Cairo soon! Tell her we may kidnap you for our museum. That will bring her here fast!" Zia laughed.

Then the four of them walked slowly away from the pyramid into the night.